COMET BOY

The First

David Perzan

D1557097

*Dedicated to my mom for inspiring me with her book, and to
Auntie Julie for helping me write and get ideas.*

Love David

CONTENTS

COMET BOY

Written and illustrated by:
11-year-old David Perzan

(With help editing from Auntie Julie)

CHAPTER 1

A not so **long time ago in a solar** system not that far away. There lived a ordinary boy, and his name was Max. BEEP! BEEP! BEEP! The alarm was ringing! "a giant asteroid is about to destroy our planet Cometverse." said the President of the solar system.

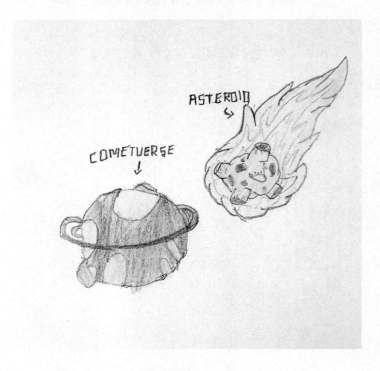

Meanwhile everyone was going cuckoo bananas running in circles... At the other side of Cometverse there was a mom and Dad and you guessed it! It was Max's Dad and Mom. They went to the last escape pod, along with Max and his sister Molly. But sadly, there was no room for the Mom and Dad, so they had to put their children in the pod alone. The Mom said, "goodbye children and I love you." and the Dad said, "you are both destined for greatness and make us proud!" The escape pod left flying to.... That is right! Planet Earth! They flew at supersonic speed! And soon they landed on Earth. They had been in the escape pod for about 11 years. While they were in space, they had to teach themselves how to walk, talk... you know all the basic stuff. When they landed, they did not really know what to do. So, they wandered around exploring this strange planet called Earth. While they were walking down the streets there was giant crowd of people. Suddenly Max heard a squeal and he looked next to him and there was a rat. When Max looked back beside him Molly wasn't there anymore! Max searched for her for hours but the more he looked for Molly, the more lost he became...

CHAPTER 2

On a different planet called Galacton an evil villain named Galacto stood in front of his masterpiece… a portal! Galacto had set up the portal so he could rule more than just his planet. Sadly, that portal led to Earth! He walked into the portal and VRRRRSSSHHHRR-ROOOOMMM!!! He was on Earth. "MWAH! HA! HA! Finally, after years of work I can take over the universe!" Said Galacto.

Meanwhile in space two brothers were going into space together named Samuel Tracker and Zeke Decker. Samuel said, "yes! we will be the first people to go onto the moon!" then Zeke said, "I get to set the first foot on the moon" and Samuel said, "no I get to set the first foot on the moon" and then they started arguing. No one was keeping an eye on where the ship was going so, they accidentally got steered into a comet shower!

They looked outside their spaceship and just sat there screaming!!! Then a comet hit the spaceship and it bounced off and started heading towards Earth…

CHAPTER 3

Meanwhile, Max was still wandering around and he looked up because he heard something. He saw a comet, but he didn't know it at first. He thought it was a shooting star, but then it got bigger and bigger and then he realized it was a comet! He ran but everyone knows you probably can't outrun a comet, unless of course you're Flash. He ran and ran and ran but it was useless, and he knew it. He thought it was the end!!! What he didn't know, was that this wasn't a normal comet it had a much different story... A couple of hours before while onboard a spaceship, an inventor named Thomas made a potion that gives you superpowers!!! He was hoping he could find someone worthy to help him create potions. Since he was getting old, he needed someone to pass on the super top-secret recipe... The potion was done, and he didn't know what to do with it or who to give it to. So, he put it on the counter next to the toilet. Which obviously wasn't a smart move. It fell off and went down the toilet!!! But Thomas did not know it had fallen and left the room. He returned a few hours later and noticed that the potion had disappeared... The potion flew into space and a comet came by at that exact moment. The comet smashed into the potion and absorbed its power. The comet hit the spaceship and bounced off heading towards Earth...
OK back to the story. Max was seconds away from being smooshed by the comet and then **CRASH!!!**

Nothing but smoke. After a while when the smoke cleared Max was still alive and feeling grateful, because somehow, he survived! He felt different and then he started floating and he realized he could fly! Just then he heard an alarm, not just any alarm, a robbery alarm! He went toward the sound of the alarm and there were bank robbers! He said, "Stop!!!" while he stuck his hand out. Suddenly his hand glowed and SHHHOOOMMM!!! A comet came out of his hand and hit the bank robbers! In that very moment he realized he could fly and shoot comets. Max realized he was a...

SUPERHERO!!!!! with actual SUPERPOWERS!!! He

was now Comet Kid.

Max returned the money to the bank, and they were happy. He went around town looking to see if anyone else was in trouble...

Nearby Galacto was walking around to check out the new planet he'd traveled to called Earth.[if you don't remember he's the bad guy in this book] "I will finally rule this planet called Earth and every other planet in the solar system!" said Galacto. Comet Kid was close by and heard everything he said. So, he followed the voice and saw Galacto. Comet Kid hovered in the air to look cool and said, "not on my watch!" Comet Kid stuck his hand out and aimed at Galacto and sure enough a comet came out and BAM! He was hit! Galacto got up and was hurt and was surprised "I thought I was going to have no challenges, but this will be more fun" Galacto said. Then he put his arms back and said, "take this!" he shot an electric beam and zapped Comet Kid. Galacto charged up his robotic hand and he punched Comet Kid in the face! He kept punching him until Comet Kid grabbed his arm while Galacto was going in for a punch. Comet Kid head-butted Galacto in the face, sending him to the ground so he could get away. Comet Kid flew up not stopping until he reached space. He needed to think of something... by then, he noticed he was in space! Comet Kid noticed he wasn't dying!? He could breathe in space which was another superpower he discovered. Which was surprising because most superheroes can't breathe in space. He sat on a nearby satellite and as he was thinking of a plan, he saw some guys in spaceship nearby. It was Zeke and Samuel, and they were in a comet shower and they needed to be saved! Comet Kid flew towards them dodging the incoming comets and he grabbed the spaceship and flew out of the comet shower saving Zeke and Samuel. While he looked back at the comet shower, Comet Kid had a great idea that might defeat Galacto...

Meanwhile, down on Earth Galacto thought Comet Kid gave up. Well that obviously wasn't the case... Galacto went back in the portal to his home planet Galacton to get his mega laser beam. He brought it to Earth and stood on a hill pointing the gun at the center of the Earth. Galacto pressed the on button and it warmed up. It was not ready yet, but in 1 minute it would be!

Comet Kid was flying back down to Earth at this very moment pushing a comet that he grabbed from the comet shower...

Galacto's mega laser beam now had only 45 seconds until it shot the beam into the Earth's core.

Comet Kid flew at supersonic speed hoping he could make it!!!

Now only 30 seconds until the laser beam fired. Galacto heard something and looked up, he saw Comet Kid pushing a comet and said: "NO!!! this will ruin my plan." Only 15 seconds left...

Comet Kid was getting closer thinking he would make it. 5.......
Comet Kid pushed will all his strength

4.......

Galacto thought he wasn't going to make it

3....... Galacto went in front of the machine and got his robotic arm ready to destroy the meteor.

2.......

Comet Kid knew his arms would break the comet, so he let go of the comet and stuck his hand out at Galacto. SHHHOOOMMMM!!!

1....... The comet that came out of Comet kid hit Galacto moving him out of the way and the speeding comet broke the mega laser beam right before it destroyed the Earth's core.

Comet Kid came out alive so did Galacto, but barely. Galacto got up coughing and said "we will meet again.... Comet Kid." Galacto went back into the portal and was gone, little did he know the portal never closed. Comet Kid realized the portal was open and didn't know whether to go in the portal to stop Galacto or just walk away. Well, he chose to walk away because he knew he was going to have more troubles.

In the portal Galacto was resting and planning his next move knowing that the next time he tried to destroy the Earth, somebody would be there to stop him and that somebody is.....................Comet Kid!

CHAPTER 4

The next morning Comet Kid woke up and went to the spot where he defeated Galacto, and the portal was still there and wide open. He thought for a second and couldn't decide if he wanted to go in and finish Galacto off, or just wait for him to return back to planet Earth. After a lot of thinking he decided to go in the portal, but Comet Kid didn't know that this was exactly what Galacto wanted… Comet Kid took a step in the portal and a couple seconds later he heard Galacto. He didn't see him he just heard him.

Galacto said "you won the battle but not the war. You will pay for yesterday when you ruined my plan…"

Just then a cage dropped on Comet Kid and tranquilizer guns were shooting at him!! Comet Kid fell fast asleep. He woke up exactly 2 hours later with Galacto standing in front of him. Comet Kid tried to punch Galacto, but he was still trapped in a cage and couldn't reach him.

Galacto said "this is going to be my payback for ruining my plan yesterday!"

"You were trying to destroy the world!" said Comet Kid.

"Guilty as charged!" said Galacto. Then Galacto said "I am working on an invention…. the mega omega laser beam!!! It will be done in approximately 15 minutes. I have already set a bomb and it will explode the whole planet of Galacton including you!" Galacto went into the portal and shut it off, so if somehow Comet Kid escaped, he couldn't get back to Earth.

The key was in front of Comet Kid on a table about 10 inches away. So, he stuck out his hand to shoot a comet, and the comet hit the table and the key fell and landed closer to him. But it was still just out of reach. So, Comet Kid looked around for something long. The longest thing he could find was a popsicle stick. So, he reached with the popsicle stick and it was just long enough to get the key closer. Comet Kid used the popsicle stick to grab the key. Comet Kid unlocked himself and noticed the bomb was about to explode the planet Galacton in 5 seconds!!! Comet Kid jumped in the air and started flying. The planet exploded just as Comet Kid left the atmosphere into space! He flew to Earth expecting the unexpected.

Comet Kid saw Galacto on the same hill but now, he had his mega omega laser beam. With only 3 minutes to go, Comet Kid had to act fast! Comet Kid had no ideas this time. His mind was blank. There was 1-minute left and Comet Kid decided to fight. He stuck his hand out at the laser beam and a comet came flying out. His aim was close but Galacto jumped in front of the beam and broke the comet with his robotic hand.

With 30 seconds left until the mega omega laser beam fired. Galacto said "this will be just like last time......except I win!"

Comet Kid had no choice but to sacrifice himself. 10 seconds until the beam fired. Comet Kid went in front of the beam and got ready for the pain.
Galacto said "NO! not this time" he got his arms ready and fired lasers out of his hands with a direct hit to Comet Kid and he was out of the way.

Now with only 3 seconds, Comet Kid got up and threw one last comet... Earth's only hope. The comet flew at the laser beam, but the comet missed, and it hit Galacto.

One SECOND TO GO... Zzzzzzzzzzzzzzzzzzzzzzz!
The laser beam fired at Earth splitting it into pieces.

With barely anything left of Earth, Comet Kid had time to go into space before the beam fired. He had failed at saving planet Earth. He didn't know what to do. He sat on a nearby satellite... again.

DAVID PERZAN

Comet Kid decided that he would rest and think about where and what to do next. He was upset Earth was gone. But at least he knew Galacto was too!

CHAPTER 5

Comet Kid looked down and saw that Earth wasn't totally destroyed... It just split into multiple pieces.

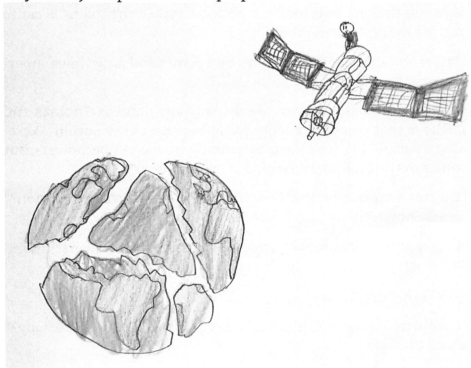

If he could get a little bit stronger maybe he could push the pieces
back together and Earth would be one again! So, that's what Comet
Kid decided to do.

Comet Kid went looking around space and soon saw a spaceship. So, he flew toward it and went inside. He flew in a little bit further and soon saw a man. The man looked confused when he saw Comet Kid. The man looked up and saw Comet Kid flying.

The man immediately thought Comet Kid had been the one who had taken his potion!

"Are you the one that took my potion?" Asked the man. "Because you are flying." the man said.

"I never took any potion. I got hit by a comet and now I have superpowers." Said Comet Kid.

"Interesting" said the man. By the way, my name is Thomas and I believe that you have superpowers because of my potion. "I created a potion that gave people the ability to have superpowers, but somehow lost it in my spaceship." Said Thomas.

"Do you happen to know how to make a super strength potion?" asked Comet Kid.

"Like a potion that makes you have super strong powers?" asked Thomas.

"Yes" said Comet Kid.

"I could make one… it might take a day or two… but I could. why?" asked Thomas.

"Because an evil villain named Galacto split Earth apart and if I was strong enough, I could push the pieces back together." Said Comet Kid."

"Okay I'll get to work, and you do superhero stuff" Said Thomas.

Comet Kid went into space and flew around. He didn't really have anything to do, suddenly he saw a light coming from one of the pieces of Earth! Discreetly he went toward it. When he looked where the light was coming from, he was surprised!!! He panicked and went back to the spaceship breathing hard....

Thomas asked, "what is wrong?" Comet Kid said "I just... I just saw... GALACTO!!!"

DUM DUM DUM... [dramatic music] "Galacto is still alive!!! I have to do something!" Said Comet Kid.

Comet Kid returned to the piece of Earth where he saw Galacto and got ready to attack him. Comet Kid shot a comet at Galacto and missed.

Galacto said "who was that?" then he saw Comet Kid. "you again? seriously?" Galacto said frustrated. Then Galacto shot a laser out of his hand and Comet Kid got knocked out falling into space.

Comet Kid fell and fell and fell... then a worm hole opened! Comet Kid suddenly woke up and saw the worm hole. Comet Kid tried to fly out of it. Comet Kid couldn't get sucked in. He was Earth's last hope!!! It was no use Comet Kid was still getting sucked into the worm hole! He shot comets into it thinking that if he fed the worm hole enough, it would close. It was working! The wormhole was getting smaller...

Suddenly Galacto appeared and said, "you are going to fall into the worm hole, and you won't be a threat to me anymore!" Galacto shot a laser beam at Comet Kid.

Comet Kid almost fell into the worm hole after being shot by a laser.
He was about 6 inches away from failure! Comet Kid threw five comets in the worm hole.

Galacto shot another laser at Comet Kid and Comet Kid was about to be defeated!

Comet Kid fell... but the comets that he had thrown in a second ago closed the worm hole! Comet Kid got up charged up his hand and punched Galacto!!! Galacto flew into space far away... but not too far away…

Comet Kid flew back to the spaceship to see Thomas. Thomas was done with the super strength potion!!! He gave it to him, and Comet Kid drank it. He could feel the power going through his veins. He shook it off and went to Earth… well what was left of it. He got a piece of Earth and pushed it with his newfound super strength! The potion was working! The pieces of Earth were coming back together! Comet Kid was so happy. He connected one piece then another. Until there was only one piece left. As he traveled toward the final piece Galacto got in the way!!!!! Comet Kid punched Galacto and **BAM!!!** Galacto was really HURT this time!!!

"Yowch!!!" Galacto said "did your hand get stronger overnight?" Comet Kid went to the last piece. He pushed the piece but then Galacto lasered him!!! The piece was moving towards Earth and it was close! Comet Kid needed just one last shove… he zoomed toward it… but Galacto got in the way and punched Comet Kid! Galacto went towards Comet Kid to punch him again but then a spaceship crashed into Galacto!!! Not just any spaceship… it was Thomas's spaceship! Galacto flew towards an asteroid shower and was long gone but we will hear from him soon…

Comet Kid gave the last push and Earth was rebuilt! But what Comet Kid didn't know, was that there was still a tiny piece of Earth not connected…

CHAPTER 6

Then out of nowhere an asteroid shower struck! It flew towards the missing tiny piece of Earth that was not connected. In that tiny piece of Earth, there was a house with a person in it!!! It was a boy and his parents had just left and he was home alone!!! The boy came out of the house and began floating away into space and he was dying... as he was floating an asteroid came and hit him!!! But this asteroid was special.............

When Thomas thought he lost his first potion, he created a second one with the same powers. Obviously, he didn't learn his lesson the first time because he set it on the counter next to the toilet again! When Thomas went to go get water the potion fell into the toilet, and it flew into space... guess what? An asteroid came by at that very moment and hit the potion absorbing its powers...

werweyeeeeeyoooo back to where we were. The asteroid hit the boy and moments later the boy could breathe!!!

"What? How is this possible? I am breathing in space!" Soon the boy realized he had superpowers. But unlike Comet Kid, this boy was a bad guy! Once the boy realized he had powers, he used them for bad instead of good. He messed up a lot of stuff by bullying people, putting elephants on skyscrapers, and setting a Giraffe on fire. The boy had decided that he needed a name... so he came up with... Dr. Asteroid! Pretty rad name am I right?

While Comet Kid was at the cape store someone crashed through the building... it was **Dr. Asteroid!**

Dr. Asteroid threw asteroids everywhere and the place was destroyed.

Comet Kid was mad because that was his favorite cape store and also the only one. Comet Kid charged at Dr. Asteroid and hit him sending him all the way to a stop sign! Dr. Asteroid's head hit the stop sign... really hard! Now Dr. Asteroid was mad!

Dr. Asteroid said, "this planet is mine!"

Comet Kid said, "I saved this planet once I can do it again!"

They started fighting... Comet Kid was losing the battle! He flew in the air and grabbed a nearby comet and threw it at Dr. Asteroid. The comet hit him and now Dr. Asteroid was mad to the max! Dr. Asteroid flew up but couldn't find Comet Kid. Then he looked toward the moon and saw a cape sticking out from behind. Dr. Asteroid flew toward the moon... Then Comet Kid kicked the moon and as it was moving through space it hit Dr. Asteroid, sending him toward Earth! Luckily, Dr. Asteroid just missed Earth!
The moon was now directly lined up with the Earth and Sun creating a solar eclipse! The Eclipse was so powerful its blasted Dr. Asteroid far away! Comet Kid had saved the day again! But did he?...

The solar eclipse had so much force it sent Dr. Asteroid towards a meteor shower. He immediately hit a meteor, sending it to the left and him to the right. The meteor flew towards a nearby asteroid shower disappearing out of sight...

CHAPTER 7

Meanwhile… Galacto was still in the asteroid shower after his previous battle with Comet Kid. Suddenly Galacto was hit by the meteor that Dr. Asteroid had earlier crashed into. This sent Galacto flying back to Earth along with the meteor…

A boy named Andrew was going for his morning walk. He didn't want to go, but his Mom Michelle told him to. Andrew was a grumpy kid. He was also a bully, and his classmates always made fun of him. He wanted revenge on them all, but he could never figure out a way how… yet. As he looked up, he saw a meteor raging toward him! He started running. "help!" said Andrew and he ran

and ran and ran. But it was useless… **Boom!**

Andrew was hit by the meteor and got knocked out… After a little while he woke up. "huh? What's going on? How am I still alive? Wait a minute I'm floating? This is just what I need! I can fly and finally get my revenge! Yes, I will get revenge on everybody! Starting with that guy all over the news… Comet Kid!"

Andrew had to come up with a name that was rad, and that name was Mr. Meteor!

Mr. Meteor searched for Comet Kid and soon saw him as he was returning back to Earth. Mr. Meteor flew toward Comet Kid and used his super strength and punched Comet Kid!

Comet Kid said, "who are you?!"

 "I'm Mr. Meteor!" Mr. Meteor said.

Comet Kid was thinking really? Dr. Asteroid? Mr. Meteor? Is this a coincidence? Then Comet Kid said "do I get a break? Now I have to defeat you too!" Comet Kid flew to space again. Mr. Meteor followed. Comet Kid spotted the moon, so he flew toward it. He formed a comet with his hand and threw it at Mr. Meteor. Mr. Meteor was now angry, and he chased Comet Kid.

Comet Kid saw Thomas and went into his spaceship and locked the doors. Mr. Meteor couldn't get in. Mr. Meteor began breaking the glass of the spaceship and Comet Kid and Thomas knew they had about 3 minutes before the glass broke.

Comet Kid asked, "can you make an anti-superhero potion?" Thomas said "yes!"

Thomas started quickly working on the potion with Comet Kid.

Mr. Meteor succeeded and broke the glass. *SHATTER!!!*

Thomas and Comet Kid were not quite done making the potion so, Comet Kid had to stall Mr. Meteor by flying around the spaceship at least 300 times! Thomas had finally finished the potion!!! Comet Kid zoomed toward the potion and Thomas held it out. While Mr. Meteor was chasing Comet Kid, Comet Kid swerved to the right and Mr. Meteor was going too fast to stop and BOOM!!! Mr. Meteor crashed into the potion! But Mr. Meteor still had his powers!

"HA! You tried to take away my powers, but it didn't work Comet Kid" said Mr. Meteor. Mr. Meteor punched Comet Kid super hard and it almost knocked him out! But then... Zzzzzzzzzzzzzzzzzzzzzzz. Mr. Meteor went for another punch but this time his super strength was gone! Comet Kid grabbed his hand and threw Mr. Meteor far away into space. He had defeated Mr. Meteor!!!

Little did Comet Kid know that Galacto and Dr. Asteroid were still alive. They were hiding on a nearby planet. Remember when I said there was a little piece of Earth that wasn't together? Well, that's where they are hiding! While they were talking, and they soon discovered that Comet Kid had defeated them both and they decided to team up. To be continued...

CHAPTER 8

4 years later Comet Kid had saved the galaxies and had been resting with no trouble from any super villains.

Dr. Asteroid and Galacto after years of work, had finished their latest invention...
Out of nowhere while Comet Kid was eating an apple, he heard a loud noise! *RUMBLE* something big was coming and fast! Comet Kid looked up and a giant robot dropped down about 10 feet away from him!!! The robot was at least ten times his size.

The robot had a ray gun, but what Comet Kid didn't know, is that it was a shrink ray! The robot shot a ray and Comet Kid ducked just in time! The robot kept shooting until he needed to reload. While the robot was reloading, Comet Kid escaped and got an idea! He flew to his house and began inventing something to defeat the

robot. After a couple of minutes Comet Kid came back and yelled "ban robots!" He even had a sign that said, "ban robots!"

The robot's gun was now recharged, and he shot another ray at Comet Kid. The ray was about to hit Comet Kid, but he flipped the sign over that said, "ban robots" and there was a mirror! The ray hit the mirror and reflected back to the robot. Zzzzzzzzzzzzzzzzzzzzzzz! The robot and his shrink ray were now Comet Kid's size. Comet Kid grabbed the shrink ray, but the robot flew away to Uranus. He used his super eyes, which he recently discovered he could do, and he used this power to see far away. He looked around 360 degrees until he saw a tiny piece of earth. He figured that's where Galacto and Dr. Asteroid would hide. Comet Kid flew to the tiny piece of Earth.

Galacto and Dr. Asteroid saw him coming and flew toward Comet Kid.

Comet Kid was so surprised! "How are you guys still alive?" he said.

Galacto said "well I…"

zzzzzzzzzzzzzzzzzzzzzzzz! Comet Kid had zapped both of them with the shrink ray while Galacto was talking. They were now really tiny, and Comet Kid couldn't see them anymore. Galacto and Dr. Asteroid took this chance and escaped…

It didn't matter anyway because what could tiny super villains do?! Well, that was a bad question… You'll see why in about 3 seconds.

CHAPTER 9

Galacto and Dr. Asteroid were tiny, which had good sides and bad sides. They used the good side to their advantage... they flew to Uranus and it took them way longer than it usually did because they were tiny. Soon they arrived on Uranus and saw the robot. They flew into the robot's chest and took over his body...

CHAPTER 10

Comet Kid was having a day off from the whole superhero thing. He was just being Max. He didn't have a mom or dad so, he lived by himself. He got himself a cup of coffee even though he was too young. Just then he heard police sirens getting closer. ——WE OO WEE OO WEE OO wee oo wee oo wee oo wee oo wee oo wee oo. He looked out his window and saw that the police were outside and about to come in.

"Max! you're under arrest! You robbed a bank and a costume shop!" said the police.

"What! I didn't do that!" said Max.

The police said, "suuuuuuuuuuure. Now come with us we are taking you to jail!" and Max was taken to the patty wagon that was waiting outside. While he was in the patty wagon Max saw a person that looked just like him across the street! Max thought that this must be the guy that was framing him! Max transformed into Comet Kid and used his super strength to bend the bars and escape from the patty wagon. The police didn't notice that Comet Kid had escaped. Comet Kid followed the guy that looked like him and said "STOP!" as he got closer, he noticed the guy was wearing a costume! Comet Kid threw a comet and the guy who was framing him fell. Comet Kid grabbed the mask and ripped it off. It was the robot with Galacto and Dr. Asteroid inside. Comet Kid got an idea and put the mask back on the robot and threw him back in the patty wagon. He used his strength to reconnect the bars. When the police returned and opened the patty wagon, they saw the villains that were the real robbers.

The police grabbed the robot by the face and discovered that it was a mask. The police realized that Max was framed by the robot wearing the costume. The police left the robot with Comet Kid and then the police took Dr. Asteroid and Galacto that were hiding inside the robot to jail. Comet Kid threw the robot with all his strength to the moon!

This was it right? Everyone had been defeated? Well pretty much... but the police weren't thinking and didn't realize, that the two bad guys were tiny and could fit through the bars! So that's just what Galacto and Dr. Asteroid did!!!

Comet Kid went to visit Galacto and Dr. Asteroid in jail, but they were gone! Comet Kid realized maybe it wasn't the smartest decision to put people the size of Legos in jail! Now Comet Kid didn't know what to do? What he didn't realize was that Galacto and Dr. Asteroid had jumped onto his head...

Galacto and Dr Asteroid thought they could hypnotize him by talking to him in his ear. Just then a policeman accidentally fell onto Comet Kid.

"Are you okay?" asked the policeman.

Comet Kid said, "I am fine."

Comet Kid left because he needed to find Galacto and Dr. Asteroid.

It turned out that when the policeman fell onto Comet Kid the evil villains ended up on the policeman! Now they were upset but at least they could still hypnotize the policeman to rob banks and, putting elephants on buildings.

Comet Kid had to come up with a plan and he had a great idea! He would shrink himself first but needed to build a grow gun first. Comet Kid knew the only way to find the evil villains was to become them! He shrunk himself with the shrink ray he used previously. Zzzzaaaappp!!! Now he was tiny and could battle them. Comet Kid went back to the Police station and flew around looking for Galacto and Dr. Asteroid. Soon he saw the policeman he talked with earlier and he was walking funny. Comet Kid noticed something on his head. There were two tiny people and Comet Kid recognized them right away! It was Galacto and Dr. Asteroid! Comet Kid reached for his grow gun and giantized the two villains. Zzzzzzzzzzzzzzzzzzzzzzz!!! They were now big. As soon as the police saw who they were, they put them behind bars! Galacto and Dr. Asteroid were now full size and back in jail, so they couldn't get out this time!

CHAPTER 11

Comet Kid used his grow gun and zapped himself, but something went wrong?! Comet Kid kept growing until he was the size of a house! He broke the walls of the jail and Galacto was now free! Comet Kid was able to step on and squish Dr. Asteroid! Dr. Asteroid had been destroyed for good!

Comet Kid had to find the shrink ray. He needed to find it and quick! Comet Kid was growing fast and at this rate he would be bigger than the Earth and would destroy a bunch of buildings, expensive cars, and most importantly people!!! Comet Kid finally spotted his shrink ray, but he couldn't grab it because he was now as tall as a big building. Also, his nose was the size of an elephant!

Comet Kid saw a boy and said, "throw my shrink ray up here!" The boy threw it and Comet Kid grabbed it. He fired the shrink ray at himself until he was the size of an normal human being. Comet Kid said "thanks kid. What's your name?"

"Sam" said the kid.

"you weren't scared. Most people would get scared and run away. But you weren't." Said Comet Kid.

"I just like saving people and doing the right thing." Said Sam.

"Tell you what. Why don't you come with me and maybe you can be my sidekick. I need some help around here." Said Comet Kid.

"Awesome!" said Sam.

Comet Kid had a great idea! He would name Sam as the new Comet Kid and he would now become Comet Boy.

"I like that name" said Sam.

"Yes Sam. This is a big responsibility. You are taking on my name as Comet Kid and you are destined for greatness!"
Comet Boy flew to Thomas because he needed a SUPERHERO potion for the new Comet Kid.

Comet Boy asked Thomas for a potion with different superpowers. Soon Comet Boy came back with the potion. "This will give you superpowers," said Comet Boy.

"Cool!" said Comet Kid and he drank the potion. *glug* *glug* *glug*.

Comet Kid wiped his mouth and flew in the air! "Whoa! I'm flying!" said Comet Kid.

"Yes!" said Comet Boy. "Your superpowers include flying, breathing underwater, teleporting, and invisibility."

Comet Kid practiced all of his superpowers until he could do it no sweat.

CHAPTER 12

Later Comet Boy returned to the jail and found out that he killed Dr. Asteroid by squishing him like jello. He also found out that Galacto got away. For some reason there was some glowing red thingy that came out of Dr. Asteroid...

Meanwhile on the planet where Galacto was hiding, he had come up with a whole new plan. He discovered that in all the galaxies there were 6 galaxy crystals!!! Comet Boy had 1, Dr. Asteroid had 1 (which explains the red glowing thingy) and Mr. Meteor had 1. The other three who had crystals remained unknown. Galacto wanted them all... because when he collects them all... the Earth would split in half!!! One side of the Earth would fly to the Sun burning everyone on that side. The other side would go to a wormhole, sucking everyone in Earth into an eternal abyss of nothingness. Galacto was determined to find the crystals to gain ultimate rulership of Earth.

Galacto went to Earth to find Comet Kid and when he did, he told him everything that I just told you about the Earth and crystals Blah! Blah! Blah! Little did Galacto know, was that Comet Kid became Comet Boy.

Comet Boy used this opportunity to trick Galacto. Comet Boy hid Comet Kid so that when Galacto left, Comet Kid could follow Galacto. Comet Boy knew he had to get all of the crystals before Galacto. Comet Boy then went to find Dr. Asteroid so he could get the Galaxy crystal before Galacto. Soon Comet Boy found Dr. Asteroid and saw the red crystal and grabbed it! Galacto flew in and zapped Comet Boy with his hands! Comet Boy flew toward a wall and banged into it. Then Galacto grabbed the crystal because it had slipped out of Comet Boy's hand when he hit the wall.

Galacto flew back to the planet Galacton 2 with the Red crystal. Comet Boy told Comet Kid to chase Galacto and get the crystal back. Comet Kid teleported to Galacto's planet and became invisible! Comet Kid arrived at the planet and he flew around until he saw the plans on Galacto's table at the laboratory. Comet Kid read what the plans said about the Earth's destruction! Comet Kid panicked and was scared, so he punched Galacto with all his might! Galacto was confused because there was nobody in the room! Galacto was hurt but he was still determined to destroy planet Earth!

Comet Kid teleported all the way back to Earth.

Comet Boy remembered that Andrew/Mr. Meteor also possessed a Yellow Galaxy Crystal... Comet Boy went into space with Comet Kid to find Mr. Meteor. He finally found him after a while of looking. But it was too late! Galacto was already there.

"Maybe next time" said Galacto. Comet Kid was furious, and he became invisible. "Where did he go?" asked Galacto. Now that Galacto couldn't see Comet Kid he used this opportunity to attack Galacto! Galacto was hurt badly so he retreated back to his base.

CHAPTER 13

Galacto already had two Galaxy Crystals and there was only four left.

Comet Boy knew just where to go for help...

"Welcome back" said King Clone. Icer, Liver and Flamer were all there too. They were the Xenergy team! It turns out King Clone had the Orange Galaxy Crystal. He used it all the time for cooking turkeys, catching fish, and setting traps. They were on Planet Clone.

Comet Boy and Comet Kid stayed with King Clone to learn the ways of the clone. They were there for a year.
Eventually Galacto found the planet that Comet Boy and Comet Kid were living on. Sadly, Galacto now had 3 Galaxy Crystals.

Comet Boy and King Clone had to protect their Galaxy Crystals because they knew that the universe was at stake!

Liver went up to Galacto and used his powers to create a weed and he whacked Galacto! Galacto was mad but he wasn't badly hurt, and he was coming straight toward King Clone! Icer approached Galacto and froze his feet. Galacto's legs were frozen and he couldn't move. So, Galacto used his lasers to get free and he grabbed Icer and was about to punch him, but Flamer came and destroyed Galacto lasers! Comet Kid joined the fight and called his ocean friend, because of his superpower that lets him talk to animals. Comet Kid called a shark and it jumped to bite Galacto, but it missed! The shark bit King Clone and he died! This made the Orange Galaxy Crystal form. Galacto used his superpowers to regrow his arms, that had been destroyed by Flamer. He then was able to grab the Galaxy Crystal. "YES!!!" said Galacto. He was happy, he now had the Orange Galaxy Crystal and flew toward Comet Boy for his Galaxy Crystal.

Comet Boy flew into space and went to Thomas's spaceship. Comet Boy said that he needed a potion and he told Thomas what he needed.

Thomas said, "I will be done in about 30 minutes."

"What!? I don't have that time" said Comet Boy.

"You'll have to wait for it if you want it to work" said Thomas.

"Fine" said Comet Boy and he flew back to Planet Clone.
Comet Boy spotted Galacto and flew towards him.
"I'm about to take your crystal" said Galacto.

"You will never take my crystal." Said Comet Boy. Comet Boy was getting impatient waiting for Thomas to finish the potion and said to Galacto, "just a second. Wait right here" Comet Boy flew to the spaceship and asked Thomas if the potion was done.

Thomas said, "I just have to add one more thing" and he finally finished the potion, and Comet Boy took it. Comet boy flew away but Thomas remembered that he had forgotten an ingredient!

"Comet Boy! Wait!" said Thomas. But it was too late, Comet Boy was gone...

Comet Boy returned to Planet Clone and had the potion with him. He smashed it on Galacto's head! Galacto went crashing down. Suddenly something happened. *RUMBLE* *RUMBLE* *RUMBLE*. The planet was rumbling! "What's going on?" said Comet Kid.

Galacto was as tall as a skyscraper and he had rad villain powers! He had invisibility, teleportation, he could shoot lasers out of his chest, and super speed movement.

Just then Thomas found Comet Boy and said "wait! Right now, it's a superhero serum with powers. I never added the anti-power ingredient that makes the powers go away!" Obviously, everyone had already noticed.

Comet Boy got an idea. "Everybody follow me" he said. So, they followed and came back later with a plan. "Hey Galacto! Over here!" yelled Comet Boy.

Galacto grabbed Comet Boy and put him in the palm of his hand. Comet Boy took out a serum and said, "I am going to drink this potion and become invincible!"

Galacto got scared and took the serum from Comet Boy and said "HA! Now I will become invincible!" and he drank the serum! ZZZZZZZZZZZZZZZZZZZZZZ Suddenly Galacto shrunk back to normal size and all of his powers were gone. "Noooooooooooo!!!" said Galacto.

Comet Boy, Comet Kid and the Xenergy team had tricked Galacto. Now they could defeat him easier. They attacked Galacto and started punching and kicking him until he was beaten to the ground! Galacto was SUPER MAD! He got back up and pointed his arms at Comet Boy. Galacto shot lasers out of his hands and they hit Comet Boy. Comet boy was knocked out and soon he started spinning and turned into a shining blue ball!!! (The "shining blue ball" was a Blue Galaxy Crystal!)

Galacto approached the Blue Galaxy Crystal and was about to grab it... but then a portal appeared out of nowhere. The portal immediately sucked the Galaxy Crystal in and then it closed!

Three seconds later, another BIGGER portal opened up and sucked up Icer, Liver, Flamer, Comet Boy, Comet Kid, and Thomas!!!

Galacto was stuck on Planet Clone all by himself.

Galacto suddenly realized that the portal that sucked all the hero's in had never closed....

CHAPTER 14

Where did they go? Well, there is a fairly good explanation. And here is what happened: So, everybody knows Midget Man right? The Superhero that can make portals appear out of nowhere and go to any place he wants. Well, Thomas had contact with Midget Man because Thomas was the one who gave him his superpowers. Thomas contacted Midget Man asked him for his help because they were losing the battle against Galacto! Midget Man came to the rescue by bringing them to his Planet...

So, where were they? Well, they were on Planet Runt. Midget Man's home planet. They were safe there... at least until Galacto came and ruined their fun.

"It's so good to see you" said Midget Man. Midget man knew how to undo The Blue Galaxy Crystal back into Comet Boy. "To change him back to his original form all you have to do, is hold him then move him up like this." *Hold* *move up* then… POP! Said Midget Man. Comet Boy was reformed, and he was back to normal.

"Thanks guys!" said Comet Boy.

"What are we going to do now?" asked Comet Kid.

"We are going to wait for Galacto and protect Comet Boy for Earth's sake." Said Midget Man.

"There is still two more crystals out there. One including mine. We have to find the other one before Galacto does." Said Comet Boy. So, Comet Boy gathered a team. "Comet Kid, Icer, and Liver. You guys will be going to find the 5th Galaxy Crystal. Flamer, Midget Man, and Thomas you guys will be protecting me." said Comet Boy.

"Let's do it!" said Flamer.

Before they left Thomas said, "I know where the fifth crystal is."

"Where?" asked Comet Boy.

"In my laboratory hidden under a towel. I use the Galaxy Crystal sometimes for my serums. That stuff is really powerful." said Thomas.

Comet Kid, Liver, and Icer went to Thomas' laboratory. But guess who else was listening? Galacto!

FYI: don't leave a portal open! Midget man just learned that the hard way.

Galacto quietly went back into the portal and flew into space to find Thomas' laboratory.

Comet Kid, Liver, and Icer arrived at Thomas' spaceship and looked around in the laboratory. Soon Icer found the towel with the Galaxy Crystal underneath.

"Found it!" said Icer.

Liver said coo-aaahhhhh! – and Liver suddenly vanished!

Somebody on the ceiling had grabbed him and pulled him up.

Comet Kid and Icer went into the laboratory. "Thomas said it was under a towel" Comet Kid said.

Icer saw the towel and said "right ther-aaahhhhh!"

Comet Kid said "Where? Icer? Liver? Where did you guys go?" Oh, look there's the towel. Comet Kid lifted the towel and under it was the Purple Galaxy Crystal!

Galacto was the mystery person who had captured Icer and Liver earlier. Galacto tied them up and threw Icer and Liver into the laboratory.

"Get the crystal and run!" yelled Icer.

Comet Kid grabbed the Galaxy Crystal and flew off.

But Galacto saw Comet Kid leaving and went after him.

Liver used his powers to make a weed grow out of the ground and capture Galacto. It grabbed Galacto but the weed was ripping!

Icer freed one of his hands and froze Galacto. Galacto's head wasn't frozen, but the rest of his body was. The ice on his body became red as the ice was warming up from the heat of Galacto's lasers. The ice on his body became redder and redder and redder until...
CRRAAACCCKKK!!

Galacto became free from the ice melting on his body, and he flew at supersonic speed towards Comet Kid. Soon Galacto caught up to him.

"Hey Comet Kid. You have something that belongs to me!" Said Galacto.

"Nuh-uh" said Comet Kid. Comet Kid used his superpowers and became invisible.

Galacto could still see Comet Kid because of how bright the Purple Galaxy Crystal was. Galacto followed the bright Purple light. Comet Kid was about to teleport. Galacto loaded his arms up with lasers and charged toward Comet Kid and zapped him. Comet Kid dropped the Crystal, and he teleported right before he could snatch it back. Galacto grabbed the crystal.

"Yes! One more crystal to go!" said Galacto. He went back to Planet Runt to get the last crystal.

CHAPTER 15

Comet Kid came back and told them what had happened. "No!" said Flamer. Suddenly they heard someone coming, the sound of a spaceship was getting closer... it was Icer and Liver!

"Galacto is coming! Be at your ready!" said Icer.

Icer, Liver, Comet Boy, Comet Kid, and Flamer saw Galacto as he epically came down from space playing an electric guitar!!!

"Ha! Ha! Ha!" said Galacto. "All I have to do is get Comet Boy's crystal and the Earth will be no more!"

"Well, that won't happen." Said Comet Boy

"Charge!!!" yelled Liver.

Flamer shot flames at Galacto, but the Yellow Crystal made a shield around Galacto! The Crystal could even protect Galacto from the Sun! Galacto used the crystal and the flames didn't have any effect on him! Then Galacto took out his latest invention...

THE INVISIBLENIATOR 3000!

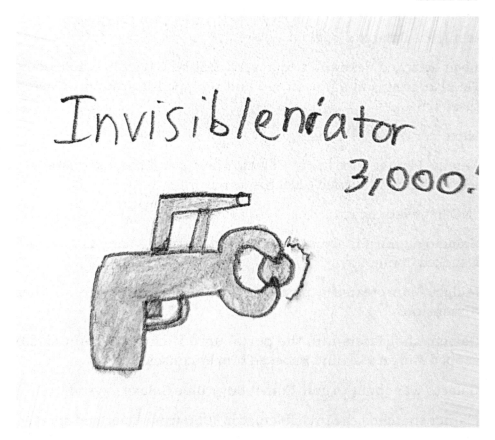

THE INVISIBLENIATOR 3000! It can make anybody invisible! The name is kind of self-explanatory.

Galacto sprayed it onto himself and he was completely gone! Then Galacto put his invention on the floor and punched Midget Man in the face. *WHAM!*

Liver saw the Invisibleniator 3000. So, he grew a plant, grabbed it, and threw the Invisibleniator 3000 to himself. Liver sprayed himself with it and he was now invisible! Liver could see everyone who was and wasn't invisible! Which meant he could see Galacto... Liver also sprayed Icer and Flamer with the Invisibleniator 3000. Now they could all see Galacto, so they attacked!!!

Icer froze Galacto's legs.

Liver attacked next and tied a weed around Galacto's whole body. He also grew some poison ivy and wrapped it around Galacto's laser arms.

Next Icer froze his arms.

Finally, Flamer shot fire at Galacto's lasers and because there was ice on them, he burned Galacto's arms off!!!

"NO!!!" yelled Galacto.

Galacto regrew his arms because of the Orange Galaxy Crystal and attacked Comet Boy.

Midget Man created a portal to suck Galacto away to another dimension.

Galacto shot lasers into the portal until it closed. Then Galacto zapped Midget Man and knocked him unconscious.

Galacto was about to grab Comet Boy's Blue Galaxy Crystal!!!

Flamer snatched the Invisibleniator 3000 from Liver and sprayed Comet Boy. Galacto couldn't see Comet Boy anymore.

"Yes!" said Flamer.
"Don't celebrate yet" said Galacto.

"Why not?" asked Icer.

"Because you forgot that I can still see Comet Boy invisible!" Said Galacto.

"Oh!" said Icer.

Galacto grabbed Comet Boy, shot a laser in his face, and took the Blue Galaxy Crystal.

"NO! WAIT!!!" said Icer.

But it was too late... Galacto put all the Crystals together. When he did particles of the crystals shot out and went to places unknown...?

KKKKKKRRRRRRRRAAAAA-AAAAACCCCCCKKKK-KKK!!!!!!!!!!!

The crystals had reacted and caused a scientifical subtropical ion-izer that resulted in a rip in the space time continuum! The Earth had then split in half!!!!!

When the crystals had combined, it split the Earth in half! One side of the Earth traveled toward a wormhole and the other side traveled toward the Sun.
Liver, Thomas, and Comet Kid were on the side of the Earth that was headed to the wormhole.

While Midget Man, Icer, and Flamer were on the side of the Earth that was floating toward the Sun. What will happen next............

CHAPTER 16

It was over. All had been lost… well…… not exactly. One side of the Earth was headed to the Sun and the other side a wormhole, right? It didn't happen instantly; it would take about 10 minutes.

Icer didn't know what to do and neither did Thomas or any of the other superheroes. All hope seemed lost… until…

"Wait a minute… a wormhole is just a giant portal." Said Liver.

"Yah so?" said Thomas.

"Which means that if we can feed it enough it can close!" said Liver.

"Hey! That might actually work! Liver! Feed it all the plants you can make, and I will make BE FULL potion. Let's do this!" said Thomas. They fed it and it was closing… but slowly…

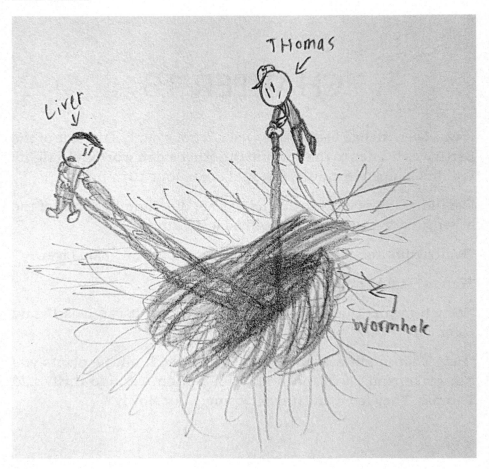

Meanwhile on the other side of the Earth...

"Hey, they are closing the wormhole. Can we close the Sun?" asked Icer.
"No, but maybe we can put it out!" said Midget Man.

"Yes! Wait...what does that mean?" asked Icer.

"It means that we will make the Sun disappear." said Midget Man.

"How will we do that?" asked Icer.

"With your powers you could probably take it out." Said Midget

Man.

So Icer put all of his Superpower into his arms and he shot ice at the Sun! The Sun was shrinking slowly... every minute that passed it shrunk an inch.

"At this rate we will be burned up before I'm halfway done" said Icer as he was losing hope.

"Keep going! I'll help you!" said Midget Man.

Midget Man started creating portals on ice planets to suck out all of the water and ice. It was going a little bit faster, but they still needed more help.

Meanwhile on the other side of Earth...

"Its closing! We will probably be done in about 1 minute 30 seconds." said Liver.

"Yeah!" said Thomas as he poured the BE FULL potions into the wormhole. Then...

"Need any help?" asked a voice.

"Who said that?" asked Thomas.

"Me" said Comet Boy.

"What!? How!?" asked Liver and Thomas.

"I guess once Galacto's used the Galaxy Crystals to split the Earth in half, we return to our original form." said Comet Boy.

"Here I'll feed the wormhole comets to help." Said Comet Boy.

Suddenly King Clone and everybody else arrived and helped to feed the wormhole and burn out the Sun. King Clone helped with the Sun because he has all of the energies... Ice, Fire, Earth, Life... So, he used the ice energy.

Soon the wormhole was closed! This was great news because they had less than ten seconds left before the wormhole sucked them up!

The other team had almost burnt out the Sun 3... 2... 1... **Boooo-ooommmmmm!!!**

It was complete darkness. Nobody could see anything...until someone saw a spark and then **FOOOMM!**
The Sun was back out but further away from where it was before. Everybody was wondering how the Sun reappeared? Somebody noticed that Flamer was gone.

Then the Sun said "hi."

"How is the sun talking?" asked King Clone.

The Sun said "guys it's me Flamer! I sacrificed myself and now I am the Sun."

"Whoa!" said Comet Boy.

"That's cool!" said Icer.

So, all the Superheroes who could fly pushed the Earth back together and just when they were about to connect... Galacto came and put his hand in the way.

"Not so fast! I have all the crystals which means one side of the Earth goes toward the Sun and the other side to a wormhole!" said Galacto.

Comet Boy and everyone else got ready for an epic battle. But they may have trouble considering Galacto is the size of Earth itself! Icer froze Galacto's foot and Galacto was having a little bit of trouble flying. Then Galacto went down because of his frozen foot.

The Superheroes tried pushing Earth together again, but Galacto's head was in the way. His head was squished by the force of both pieces of Earth connecting!!!

Galacto was now out of the way and the Superheroes could reconnect the Earth!

"YAY!" said all the superheroes and Flamer who was now the Sun.

Galacto got mad and zoomed straight towards Earth hoping to crash into it and destroy everything.

Midget Man saw Galacto and created a giant portal in front of Earth. Galacto was going so fast that he couldn't stop himself and he flew into the giant portal instead. Guess where that portal led to...? The SUN!

"NO!!!" Galacto screamed. Galacto was destroyed. Or was he...

CHAPTER 17

They did it! They defeated Galacto by throwing him into the Sun. But I still have a lot of pages to go, so let's see what happens next...

There is a couple more bad guys. You ready? Its origin story time! There once was a boy named Michael. He was a good boy. Always doing his homework. Cleaning his room without being told.

His dad always said, "your SUPER!"

His mom would say "you're like a bright shining NOVA!"

The boy loved that name, and he made his name Super Nova! He even created a costume. His superpowers were being nice, gener-

ous... that kind of stuff. But then one day... KKKKK-RRRRRRAAAAAACCCCCCKK-KKKKK!!!!!!!!!!!

The Earth split in two and his parents were sucked into space. Gone forever. From then on, he vowed revenge on whoever did it! When he looked outside, he saw Comet Boy and his super strength and thought he was the one who did it and got to work. He built a spaceship and flew to Thomas's laboratory. He had heard that Thomas was an expert potionist. Super Nova forcefully made Thomas create a superpower potion for him.

Super Nova with his new superpowers sought out to find Comet Boy and destroy him… Who knew such a good guy could become such a bad guy? Anyways back to narrating…

Meanwhile on planet Earth…

"Thanks for all of your help" said Comet Boy.

"Your welcome" said all of the superheroes that helped him defeat Galacto and restore peace throughout the land.

It was back to just Comet Boy. The solo fighter because Comet Kid wanted to go with Midget Man to his planet.
Then after everyone was gone. *BOOM!* Comet Boy looked around until he saw a boy.

"You! Your Comet Boy, right?" asked the boy.

"Why yes I am" said Comet Boy proudly.

The boy who was known as Super Nova then formed a nova with his hands and threw it at Comet Boy. It hit Comet Boy and he couldn't move. He was stunned! This froze him for 7 seconds. Super Nova punched Comet Boy in the face.

"Owwww!" said Comet Boy.

"I am Super Nova. Ruler of all the galaxies" said Super Nova.

Comet Boy said "Well I'm sorry but the galaxies are protected by me. Comet Boy."

Super Nova threw another nova at Comet Boy. Comet Boy ran as the nova was getting closer. Then Comet Boy saw the jail and remembered the last time he battled the robot.

Comet Boy ran towards the jail and looked for the sign with the mirror he used to defeat the robot on page 9. Comet Boy found the sign and he flipped it over to the mirror side and the nova bounced back at Super Nova.

Boom! It hit Super Nova and he was stunned. Comet Boy flew towards him and POW! Comet Boy punched Super Nova sending him to the ground. Super Nova was now un-stunned and was terribly angry! Super Nova's eyes turned yellow and there was an electric nova beam all around him. He used the beam as a weapon by crossing his arms to send it across the whole world, stunning everyone including Comet Boy!!!

While Comet Boy was stunned Super Nova grabbed him and brought him to his secret lair. It was located under a restaurant. Super Nova locked Comet Boy in a cell. Super Nova took the keys and swallowed them to make sure Comet Boy didn't escape.

Comet Boy became un-stunned because the electric nova beam had worn off. Comet Boy saw Super Nova eat the keys and where he was standing near the cell.

Super Nova said "I am going to rule planet Earth and make everyone my slave. I will order them to attack and destroy every other planet in the solar system!"

Suddenly Super Nova had a stomachache and barfed in a trash can right next to Comet Boy. At one point when he was barfing, he had trouble getting something out of his throat. Then Super Nova left to start his evil plan.

The trash can fell over because it was so heavy from the barf. Suddenly Comet Boy spotted something shiny. So, he looked closer and Super Nova had barfed up the keys! Comet Boy grabbed the keys avoiding the puke. Then he unlocked the door of the cell and flew to rescue Earth from Super Nova's evil plan...

CHAPTER 18

Comet Boy eventually spotted Super Nova and tried to think of a plan. Soon he got an idea.

"Hello citizens. I am Super Nova. Evil criminal mastermind! And you will now be all of my slaves." Everyone was scared until…

"Do not fear! Comet Boy is here!" said Comet Boy.

"What!? How did you escape?" asked Super Nova.

"Be careful what you barf" said Comet Boy.

The battle was on!!!

Super Nova shot a nova at comet boy. Comet boy dodged it and then he attacked Super Nova and punched him. Comet Boy punched Super Nova again! Super Nova got mad and his eyes started to turn yellow. Comet Boy knew where this was going so, he reacted quickly. He grabbed Super Nova and flew into space. Then Comet Boy saw Midget Man.

Midget Man said, "everybody on my planet just froze."

Then Super Nova was about to erupt!

"Can you create a portal please?" Comet Boy asked.

Midget Man made a portal like Comet Boy had asked him.

Comet Boy threw Super Nova in the portal right before he stunned everybody with his Electric Nova beam!

"Need any help with this guy?" asked Midget Man.

"Well, I could use a little help. Ok here's my plan." Said Comet Boy. *whisper* *whisper* *whisper*

CHAPTER 19

Soon Super Nova found his way back to Earth. While he was in the portal, he had created a new invention... THE STUNNER 4000! Your probably not wondering what it does because the name pretty much gives it away. Once Super Nova fires it up it will stun the whole planet for 10 minutes unless, somebody is currently walking through a portal. Super Nova fired it up... 3...

Meanwhile on Earth. "Okay Midget Man let's put our plan into action" said Comet Boy. Midget Man made a portal.

... 2...

"You go first" said Midget Man.

... 1...

Comet boy stepped in the portal just as the beam from the Stunner 4000 fired across the whole Universe!
Zzzzaaaappp!!!

Comet Boy reached the other side of the portal. "Midget Man... Midget Man are you coming?" asked Comet Boy.

Then the portal closed. Suddenly Comet Boy realized everyone was frozen. He knew who did it too. Super Nova! So, he went looking for Super Nova and finally saw him and The Stunner 4000. Then when Super Nova wasn't looking, Comet Boy flew towards the Stunner 4000 and since he was a tech genius, he reversed the affect!

Super Nova said "I am going to fire the Stunner 4000 a million times so nobody will ever bother me again. Then he fired it. 3...
2... 1... Zzzzaaaappp!!!

Suddenly everybody was unstunned and moving again!

"Huh?" said Super Nova.

Then...PA-POW! Comet Boy hit Super Nova. Super Nova was knocked out from Comet Boy's punch. While Super Nova was unconscious, Comet Boy messed with the Stunner 4000 and added a tweak.

Soon Super Nova woke up. He pushed the button on the Stunner 4000.

3... 2... 1... Zzzzaaaappp!!!

Everybody was still moving. But guess who wasn't? Super Nova! He was the only person still stunned. Comet Boy grabbed the Stunner 4000 and pressed the button a bunch of times, then threw Super Nova as far as he could into space!... About a minute later he broke the Stunner 4000 and heard a little zap...

Comet Boy flew to find Midget Man who was still on Planet Earth and told him everything that happened with Super Nova.

Midget Man returned to his home planet: planet Runt.

Origin Story time! So, there was this boy named Leon and he was good in general. But he was really mischievous. He liked to steal people's money, talk back to adults, and bully people. Then one day a black hole opened, and his planet was really close to it. Leon held on for dear life, but his parents got sucked in and his sisters and one of his brothers. Leon still had 2 brothers left that were safe.

 The wormhole closed right before they were about to get sucked in. Leon was really mad. He wanted revenge on whoever had opened that wormhole and guess who he saw after that? Comet Boy! Now he knew who was responsible for this mess! Leon named himself after the very thing that sucked his parents up into the Black hole. Sergeant Black Hole.

Next, Sergeant Black Hole/ Leon went to Thomas's spaceship because he had heard that he was an expert potionist. Sergeant Black Hole snuck in and took a serum…

Sergeant Black Hole flew around all of the planets looking for Comet Boy. He spotted a superhero flying around and thought it was Comet Boy…

CHAPTER 20

Meanwhile on planet Runt…

"I love running this planet" said Midget Man.

"You are a good leader" said Comet Kid.

…BEEEEP! BEEEEP! BEEEEP! The alarm is ringing.

"Someone has entered the atmosphere." said Comet Kid.

Just then Sergeant Black Hole showed up.

"Hello everyone" said Sergeant Black Hole.

"Hi. Who are you?" said Midget Man.

"I'm about to take over your planet!" said Blackhole.

"Sorry I can't let you do that" said Midget Man.

"Oh yes you can." Said Blackhole.

Suddenly an army of robots came and captured everyone. The robots tied everyone up and set fires everywhere! The planet was going to be no more soon. But Midget Man threw a portal at Blackhole and he missed.

"Ha you missed!" said Blackhole.

"I wasn't aiming for you" said Midget Man.

Then on planet Earth a portal opened in Comet Boy's house and he went in it… when he went in, he saw all the burning fires! Blackhole saw Max and knew that he was Comet Boy. Then Blackhole left the planet.

Comet Boy untied Midget Man and they escaped before Planet

Earth burned down. Suddenly Midget Man remembered that his parents were still on the planet, so he went to rescue them. Midget Man saw his parents and flew towards them but then...

BOOOOOMMMMM!!!

The planet exploded... Midget Man was killed!!!
"Noooo!" yelled Comet Boy.

Suddenly a wormhole opened and sucked Planet Runt up, never to be seen again!

Comet Boy didn't know what to do. His best friend was gone. His sadness turned to madness!!! He wanted to defeat Sergeant Blackhole for the death of his friend. He flew into outer space to find him. He finally spotted him on Earth. Comet Boy started walking toward him. Then Boom!!! Comet Boy was hit by something and was frozen. Then he became unfrozen 5 seconds later.

"What was that?" asked Comet Boy.

Out of nowhere Super Nova appeared in front of Comet Boy.

Okay you are probably like what is going on? I thought Super Nova was frozen forever. Well, if that's what you think you obviously don't pay attention to my clues. Okay so let's rewind a little. So, in Chapter 19 it says "So, Comet Boy pressed the button a million times then threw Super Nova as far as he could. About a minute later he broke the machine. He heard a LITTLE ZAP when he broke it." Your probably still like... I still don't get it. Well Comet Boy destroyed the machine, right? Which means the effect was destroyed because it came from that machine. So, the "little zap" was that the effect was gone, and Super Nova was now unfrozen. It took him a little while to find his way back to Earth. So anyways back to where we were... Super Nova was in front of Comet Boy. Then Comet Boy said, "I guess I will have to defeat both of you."

So Super Nova and Blackhole attacked Comet Boy. Comet Boy panicked threw a comet and flew to Thomas's crib/house/rad spaceship. Because that's where he goes when he panics. Super Nova and Blackhole were coming in fast!

"I need you to make a potion that morphs two people together. I will morph myself with a robot and be unstoppable!!!" said Comet Boy.

Then Super Nova and Blackhole appeared in front of the window of the spaceship. Super Nova and Blackhole started to break in so, Comet Boy and Thomas only had about 3 minutes until they were inside the spaceship.

"Hurry!" said Comet Boy.

Now there was only 1-minute left until they broke in! Finally, Thomas had finished the potion with only 30 seconds to spare! Comet Boy warmed up and he was ready to drink the potion when... *SHATTER* the window broke!

Super Nova and Blackhole were now in the spaceship and flying toward Comet Boy. Comet Boy grabbed the potion held it up and got ready to drink it... When suddenly Super Nova and Blackhole crashed into him. Then when everybody got back up Comet Boy saw Super Nova who looked different, but he didn't see Blackhole? Then Comet Boy realized his potion was gone. When he looked at Super Nova, he realized what happened! When they crashed into him, they both crashed into the potion and got morphed together which would make him: Sergeant Nova!

Now Sergeant Nova had all of the powers of Blackhole... in addition to his villain powers now he could make black holes appear, fly, and breathe in space.

CHAPTER 21

Sergeant Nova attacked Comet Boy and grabbed him.
"Nice try. But now I'm unstoppable!" said Sergeant Nova.

"Give me the backup potion" said Comet Boy and Thomas handed him the extra potion he had made earlier. Comet Boy poured it all over Sergeant Nova. Suddenly Sergeant Nova didn't have any powers and he couldn't see!

"Argh! Where is everybody?" said Sergeant Nova.

"Quick! Give me the backup backup potion!" said Comet Boy. Thomas threw him the extra extra potion that he had made earlier and poured it onto Sergeant Nova.

Super Nova now looked like himself and Blackhole was right next to him separately. Blackhole got so confused he just opened up a wormhole and left...

Then it was just Comet Boy and Super Nova.

"Give me your best shot" said Comet Boy.

Super Nova said, "okay if you say so."

Super Nova created a giant nova, and it was as big as a 7-foot human.

Super Nova aimed it at Comet Boy got ready to shoot... then he fired. It barely missed Comet Boy and it went off to somewhere unknown.

Comet Boy said to Thomas "make a read - people's - mind potion."

So, Thomas got right to work.

Super Nova made another nova and shot it at Comet Boy. This time it hit him!

Comet Boy was frozen for 5 seconds and Super Nova charged up his hand and uppercut Comet Boy.

"Ouch!" said Comet Boy.

Comet Boy got back up and he zoomed toward Thomas.

"The serum! Now!" said Comet Boy.

Thomas tossed Comet Boy the serum and he caught it! So, he drank half of the serum and looked at Super Nova. Super Nova was thinking... I will turn invisible sneak up behind Comet Boy and punch his back so hard he'll faint!

Comet Boy knew what he was going to do to defend himself because he knew what Super Nova was thinking. A moment later Super Nova became invisible. When Comet Boy thought Super Nova was behind him, he turned around and punched him right in the gut and became visible! Comet Boy saw him, and grabbed him, knocked him out and flew back to Earth. Comet Boy put him into supervillain jail where he belonged.

Super Nova's plan was foiled. Hooray for Comet Boy!!!

CHAPTER 22

Remember when I said Super Nova/Michael had 2 brothers? Well, they both watched on TV what had happened to their brother and that's when they became angry!!! They created their own names, and costume's. They were now: Astro Kid! and Star Boy! Yes, they sounded like good guys, but they weren't. So, anyways they wanted payback on Comet Boy for putting Super Nova/ Michael, their brother, in jail. So, they studied all kinds of science in order to create an invention to defeat Comet Boy. Soon after a couple days they were masters at inventing.

They knew everything from $1+1$ to $E=Mc2$! They created an invention, and it was called: The Choose-you-Fuse 4000

The way it works is that you can choose 2 superpowers and have them injected into your hand. There IS a potential for a 3rd superpower, but that slot hasn't been tested yet.

So anyway, Astro Kid had the injection first. He chose flight and mind reading. Zzzzzzzzzzzzzzzzzzzzz now he had those superpowers and tested them out.

"Think of something" said Astro Kid.

So, Star Boy thought of 2 milkshakes with Oreo flavoring.

Astro Kid asked, "are you thinking of 2 milkshakes with Oreo flavoring?"

Star Boy was amazed! His invention had worked!

"Yes! that was what I was thinking!" said Star Boy.

Then it was Star Boy's turn. He chose flight and super strength/big muscles. Zzzzzzzzzzzzzzzzzzzzz now Star Boy had those powers and he tested them out. Once they knew for sure they had superpowers they flew to find Comet Boy.

Meanwhile Max/Comet Boy was at home chilling.

He had a stressful, overwhelming day. So, he was happy to finally relax. Then he heard a noise. "MWA! HA! HA!" He was upset. "Come on! I need to rest! Now what is it?! The he heard them say.

"We are two bad guys with awesome superpowers that can take over the world!"

That was the last straw for Max! He didn't know what to do. Fight them and save the world… again. Or stay home rest and feel bad knowing the world is getting destroyed this instant and he could've saved it… After a lot of thinking he decided that he would do the right thing and go battle the two bad guys. Comet Boy left his house and saw the chaos everywhere! It wasn't too bad. On a scale of meh to chaotic how would you rate this chaos? Comet Boy rated it a 4: bad.

Comet Boy flew up to them and yelled, "get out of here!"

Astro Kid and Star Boy immediately noticed Comet Boy. Astro Kid read Comet Boy's mind as he was thinking: I need sleep.

"He needs sleep." said Astro Kid.

"Good we'll use that to our advantage." Said Star Boy.

So, they went to a store and stole a comfy blanket and a pillow. Star Boy spun around Comet Boy till he was completely wrapped in the blanket. Then Comet Boy fell, and Astro Kid put the pillow under his head, and he fell asleep in an instant. Astro Kid got a sword out of his pocket and held it up getting ready to kill Comet Boy...

WOAH!!! okay let's pause right there. Your probably like how are you going to finish the book if your only on the 29th page? Well... do you remember in chapter 21 when Super Nova made a giant nova as tall as a 5-foot human? Well, it missed Comet Boy and went somewhere unknown right? Well, that unknown place was Earth. So anyway, lets continue to where we were...

Astro Kid was about to destroy Comet Boy... but then it became dark. Star Boy and Astro Kid looked up and saw a giant nova! (a nova is technically a type of star by the way) then the nova smashed into Star Boy and Astro Kid. SMASH!!!

The nova just missed Comet Boy! It was so loud Comet Boy woke up. But this time he had a good sleep, and his energy was full! Soon he saw Star Boy... but not Astro Kid? Then he saw him on the ground... Star Boy was alive and moving but Astro Kid was not.

"NO! you killed him" said Star Boy.

"What I didn't kill him" said Comet Boy.

"Yes, you did!" yelled Star Boy.

Soon his sadness turned into madness. He got mad. Real mad. So, he charged at Comet Boy.

"Uh-oh" said Comet Boy.

Comet Boy flew up into space and Star Boy followed behind. Comet Boy arrived at a random planet. (it was Star Boy's planet) He saw The Choose-You-Fuse 4000 in front of him. He saw three slots with a keypad and typed random letters. (hint: Star Boy hasn't tested the 3rd slot yet.) Suddenly Star Boy came out of nowhere and grabbed the Choose-You-Fuse 4000, but he didn't know it was running. By the time he noticed it was too late. Zzzzzzzzzzzzzzzzzzzzzzzz!
It's not all that complicated to say what happened... The third slot was actually a reverse slot! Which means if you have powers it reverses them.

"No!" said Star Boy who was now just Joshua.

So, Comet Boy took him to jail. Yay! The world is saved for the ninth time! Maybe more! But there is still a lot of pages to go and why do I keep telling you how many pages are left? Well anyway are you guys ready for another story? If you said no, too bad.

CHAPTER 23

So, Astro Kid had a good friend named Isaac. He was just chilling out eating ice cream watching tv... until the tv announced that Astro Kids friend Eric dies because of a giant comet or something...

When Isaac heard about that, it was news to him. Then he remembered what the lady said, "giant COMET or something." So, he thought for a moment and suddenly thought of Comet Boy. He literally had comet in his name! so he thought that he had killed him. Obviously if you remember it was a nova. But because the news lady isn't a meteorologist or fascinated in science... she said "comet." Well anyways back to where we were... Isaac lived on the same planet as his friend. (Eric) so he went to Eric's house to see if he could find anything useful. Then he saw something, it looked like an invention.

On the top it was labeled "The Choose-you-Fuse 4000!" After a

little while of reading the instruction manual. He finally knew how to use it. He chose the option to read people's minds, and also teleport. So, he tried it out and teleported to Earth (with the invention).

Then he landed right in front of Comet Boys house... meanwhile... inside Comet Boys house. Max was getting himself a treat. Not like a doggy treat. But a cookie. It was on the top shelf. He couldn't reach it even with his tippy toes. So, he hovered in the air just a little bit and grabbed the cookie jar. And he started eating cookies. "these are delicious." Said Comet Boy.

Then Solar Man(Isaac) broke in.

"Hey dude you just broke my roof!" said Max.

"Oops. I guess I did." Said Solar Man. Then Solar Man used his powers to tell what Comet Boy was thinking. What Comet Boy was thinking was "I'm going to fly up punch him then uppercut him." Now Solar Man knew what he was going to do.

So, Comet Boy flew up and went to punch Solar Man, but Solar Man knew it was coming. Solar Man grabbed Comet Boys hand when he was about to punch him, and he twisted his fist. Then Comet Boy went to uppercut Solar Man but again, Solar Man knew it was coming. So, he dodged it and Solar Man punched Comet Boy in the gut.

"argh!" said Comet Boy.

Solar Man thought of what Comet Boy was thinking... then Comet Boy used the same power to read Solar Man's mind... then Comet Boy thought what Solar Man was thinking and Solar Man thought what Comet Boy was thinking. Then what they thought was thinking what Comet Boys thinking that he's thinking about me thinking that I'm thinking about him thinking about what I'm going to say.

Okay. That was a little bit confusing! But don't worry because from now on it should be a whole lot simpler. Then Comet Boy flew in the air and Solar Man chased him for a while... until something fell out of Solar Man's pocket. It was the invention!

Comet Boy recognized the invention, and he went after it. So did Solar Man. Comet Boy grabbed it just in time and Solar Man chased after him! He was gaining on him! So, Comet Boy thought of what he did last time to beat Star Boy... he remembered that if he chooses 3 things then it reverses the powers. So, Comet Boy chose 3 things on the invention. Then he handed it to Solar Man. Then the Choose-You-Fuse 4000 was vibrating.

Solar Man was scared so he threw it in front of Comet Boy. then Comet Boy caught it. Comet Boy tried to throw it, but it was too late. Zzzzzzzzzzzzzzzzzzzzzz! Comet Boy fell to the ground. He was about to fly up and punch Solar Man really hard! But then... he was unable to fly. He got confused so he stuck out his hand to shoot a comet... but nothing came out? Comet Boy... had lost his superpowers.

Wow! that's crazy! You are probably like, "How did that happen?" Well, it's kind of simple if you paid attention to Chapter 22. So, the invention was that you could enter 2 superpowers of any choice. But the 3rd slot hadn't been tested yet. Remember?

So, the 3rd slot was actually the opposite of all of them. So that meant if you entered anything in the 3rd slot... all of your powers would get sucked into there. You might not get it yet. So, let's go a little bit further in detail... So, Comet Boy remembered that he defeated the other bad guys by putting something in the 3rd slot. So that's what Comet Boy did. He put 3 things in and threw it at Solar Man. But Solar Man got scared so he threw it in front of Comet Boy. Comet Boy accidentally caught it and it zapped him... so do you get it now? Comet Boy lost his powers. That's why he couldn't fly or shoot comets.

Okay now back to where we were... "What? Why aren't my powers working?" asked Comet Boy. he didn't pay attention to anything I just said.

"You lost them" said Solar Man. "Looks like your plan backfired!" said Solar Man. "MWA! HA! HA!"

"No!" said Comet Boy. Comet Boy had it all figured out now. He couldn't fly to Thomas. The only thing he could do was get the invention that started it all... The-Choose-You-Fuse 4000.

Solar Man flew up to the moon and dug a hole. Then he put the invention in the hole and covered it. Comet Boy couldn't fly anymore. comet boy could... wait a minute. What's happening to the word. Whenever I say comet boy it shrinks... wait a minute. Since comet boy isn't a superhero anymore. that's not his name. so now he's plain... Max. No this can't happen or the whole book will disappear! comet boy needs to do something before everything is gone........

Wait I am coming back. What happened? I guess _has an idea! that was close. I thought the book was about to be over. But let's see Max's idea... "I can make an invention!" said Max. "I just have to create a Rocketship."

CHAPTER 24

4 MONTHS LATER...

"I am done with the invention!" said Comet Boy. "Nothing bad can happen now" wow okay. JSYK(just so you know) never say stuff like that. Just then a blackhole appeared... then someone came out of the blackhole... it was Sergeant Blackhole! It may be hard to remember but back in CHAPTER 21 he creates a blackhole and gets away. He ended up right next to Comet B-err I mean Max. what a coincidence. Comet Boy couldn't defeat him, so he went to the spaceship. And he took off! "10,9,8,4,3,2,1..." "what happened to 7,6 and 5?" asked Max. "liftoff!" vvvvrrrrrsssshhhrrrooomm!!! And the Rocketship took off!

Blackhole looked in the window and saw Max. so he flew up and followed Max. but the rocket ship was way faster than Blackhole, so he was like 2 minutes behind. So, the rocket ship landed on the Moon. He put on his helmet and went to where Solar Man was. Then he saw the hole and Solar Man too. He didn't want Solar Man to see him.

So, he snuck into the hole. Then Max saw that the hole was human size, and it wasn't that deep. So, he went in. he saw the invention and put 2 superpowers in the slot. He pressed the submit button... but then it didn't work. He looked at the top left and there was a sign that said "LOW BATTERY" so now Max needed new batteries. He didn't know where to get batteries... then he remembered the robot... In CHAPTER 10 he threw the robot on the Moon! If he could find the robot, take its batteries, and fix the invention and get his powers back he could save the world!!!

So, he got out of the hole quietly and looked around until he saw the robot. He stuck his hand out to shoot a comet, but he remembered he didn't have that power anymore. So, he charged at the robot and tackled the robot. He took the batteries out and put them in his pocket. Then he snuck back in the hole.

So, he put the batteries in and put in his 2 superpowers. Flying and comets coming out of your hand. Then... Zzzzzzzzzzzzzzzzzzzzzzz! Comet Boy was back to normal! Then Solar Man came to the hole held open the flap and **BAM!** Comet Boy had punched him really hard! So, then Comet Boy flew out of the hole and grabbed Solar Man. Swung him round and round... and then he threw him to Earth. Meanwhile Sergeant Blackhole was just coming up on Comet Boy when he saw something spinning and coming towards him fast!

Then Solar Man hit Blackhole, and they both got knocked out. When they woke up, they were in jail with their powers gone. Because Comet boy had used the Choose-You-Fuse 4000 to take away their powers and then he took them to jail.

"No fair." Said Solar Man.

"Yeah." Said Blackhole, and then Comet Boy left. Comet Boy had done a lot. He saved the world from countless bad guys... I am so sad that this book is ending in 8 pages. I just want to cry. But not really. Don't worry though. There is a 99.999999999999% chance that I will make a 2nd Comet Boy book. So be excited!

Anyways there is 1 more bad guy maybe 2 that we have before we end this book. So, remember in CHAPTER 16 when Galacto was put in a portal that went to the sun? Well remember the yellow galaxy crystal? In CHAPTER 15 it says in large letters... that it "makes a shield around you. And it could even PROTECT YOU FROM THE SUN!" do you remember that? So that means Galacto can use the yellow galaxy crystal to protect himself from the sun and come back to Earth. But what are the chances that that will happen? RUMBLE!!!!! ZAP!!! A portal appeared. Galacto was standing there!!!

He walked toward Comet Boy but tripped on a rock.

"Ouch!" said Galacto. Then he got up and said "HA! HA! HA! Daddy's home!" But Comet Boy didn't know that Galacto was still alive. So that was bad. But the worst part is that Galacto is coming for Comet Boy. Galacto wanted to defeat Midget Man first because well he's the one who sent him into the sun. but as we know... Midget Man... isn't alive anymore. so, he went after Comet Boy because he was the main person that gathered everyone up to defeat him. So, he went around looking for him... meanwhile Max was in his house. He was making pierogies. (the best food in the universe) So soft and crunchy!!!

... anyways he sat at the table and started eating. Soon after Comet Boy was done, he washed his plate and went outside for a walk. Then he went into the town. He liked walking around town and greeting neighbor's good afternoon.

So, he went into a restaurant. He needed a drink. So, he ordered a lemonade. But what Comet Boy didn't know was that Galacto was sitting in a booth behind him. What are the chances they were in the same restaurant? Surprisingly good actually because we're running out of pages. So anyways the waiter came to Comet Boys table and asked him if he wanted something to drink.

Comet Boy asked "may I have some chips and a PB and J."

"Right away sir" said the waitress. Comet Boy and Galacto both ordered a lot of food!

CHAPTER 25

AN HOUR LATER...

They both finished eating and the waitress asked Galacto. "Are you ready for the bill? Mr.... how do you pronounce that name?"

"Galacto." Said Galacto.

Once Comet Boy heard that name he almost choked on his remaining chips. So, Comet Boy looked over the booth and saw Galacto.

"This isn't possible." Said Comet Boy.

Then Galacto walked to the EXIT. Comet Boy had to do something fast! So, he shot a comet out of his hand and it hit Galacto. BOOM

"Ow!" said Galacto.

"That was a comet... Comet Boy is here."

Then Galacto looked behind him and saw Comet Boy run into the bathroom. So Galacto followed him. Comet Boy hid in the farthest stall to the right. Galacto kicked open the first stall. Nothing... Then he kicked open the second stall. Nothing... Then he got ready to kick the last stall...

Comet Boy crawled under the stalls and kept crawling until he was out. Then he left the bathroom.

So, Galacto kicked open the third stall. Nothing... He knew he had gotten away somehow?! So, he looked outside the bathroom and saw Comet Boy just as he was getting away. Now the battle had begun. Galacto flew out the building and he saw a girl wandering around looking lost. Then he saw Comet Boy.

"It's over now!" said Galacto.

"Or is it?!?" said Comet Boy as he flew in the air and charged at Galacto while Galacto charged at him....

TO BE CONTINUED... in the next book...

ACKNOWLEDGEMENT

Special thank you to Auntie Julie for encouraging me, helping me edit the book on zoom for weeks and weeks and for being the best Auntie and cookie maker!
Thank you to my mom for inpiring me to make a book like you did. (You can look up her books - Michelle Perzan!)

ABOUT THE AUTHOR

David Perzan

 David Perzan lives in Cypress, Texas with his family and is going into grade 8 and is 13 years old. He wrote Comet Boy when he was 11 and his dream was to publish it and become and author.

You can find David drawing comics, looney toon characters and dinosaurs for fun, watching tv (Family Ties is one of his favourites from the past) and playing video games and lego Mario.

His goal is to continue to write and illustrate books to make people laugh and be creative with new superheros!

Made in the USA
Columbia, SC
19 August 2021